As the Darkness Dawns

(An Anthology of Dark Poetry)

Dr. Ujjwala Kakarla

Published by InkQuills Publishing House
www.inkquills.in

First Edition 2022

ISBN: 978-93-90567-12-6

Foreword

Suffering has always been inseparable part of worldly affair, be it loss, unfavourable circumstances, separation or death. Language is not enough to explain how the shades of dark time occupy the human psyche erasing all the colours of happiness and hollows the heart. The despair, pain and grief drag one forcefully into the blackhole of trauma. Only a few of us dare to explore the potential of dark to bridge the light within us. **As the Darkness Dawns** is an anthology of dark poetry, written by Dr. Ujjwala Kakarla, a prominent scholar and an author of several books on various disciplines. I have known her as a person with high morale and tremendous dedication towards her profession. Her poems are graceful blend of philosophy, intellect and emotion. In this collection of 70 poems, layers of human fear, stress, poverty, suffocation, mourning the death of beloved ones, pain of the dark feelings and the struggle to overcome all these is expressed in a simple language, yet the diction is aesthetically rich.

In the poem, **A Tribute to My Beloved Amma,** the poet pays homage to her late mother. It displays the overwhelming effect of her demise upon her. It's a lamentation of the irreparable loss of the big support of life. Instead of shedding tears like ordinary people, the poet is bold to express her tribute and gratitude to the departed soul with an oath to walk on her footprint. ***An Empty Nest*** presents the pitiful condition of baby birds after the mother bird leaves her nest reflecting the significance of Mother on the earth. Since the primitive age, man has carried the death as a horror and mystery. ***A wooden Boat Under the Wild Sky*** portrays the shattered lives of the near ones and of the deceased. ***Ocean of Death*** is a visualization of man on death bed battling to leave the worldly attachments. ***Nature Intact*** reveals the immense power of nature motivating mankind to face the day today hazards with tolerance and courage. ***How Small are our Lives*** points out the plight of daily wage workers stuck in the cities to earn their livelihood, but could not be with their families during the pandemic. The poverty-stricken folk with little work longing and struggling to leave the cities on one hand, the fear of the serpentine virus hissing in rage biting one after the other victim on the other hand, the government being helpless and hopeless to save the lives of victims, overall, a chaotic and dreadful situation in battle with mankind's emotions and reactions reflect the prevailing scenario then with a tone of empathy.

In the poems, ***The Hell of Darkness***, ***Those Dark Hours*** and ***In the Eyes of Dark World***, she voices against how the time of despair, grief and senseless remarks and actions of wicked people try to wound and harm her gentle self. Amidst the inner jungle of heavy emotions, she is all alone, yet fighting a non-violent battle defending herself from these ignorant souls. Here, the middle path, being neutral to observe the happenings and possibilities to modify the thoughts is discovered, the germination of positive thoughts and life growing out of it can be closely observed, the existence of hope and presence of natural beauty is also recognized. But it is the same darkness that can be a transit point towards awakening. The poet depicts the connection between the darkness and spiritual growth stimulating the mankind to endure pain with patience. These poems remind me of Buddha saying, "Appo Deepo Bhava"- be a light onto yourself, so too, the poet motivates to search one's own light within. *As The Darkness Dawns* from which the book received its' title is a symbolic poem which reveals how the evil thoughts allure our sub-conscious and how they could be filtered without getting arrested. *The Chaotic Mind, The Seeds I Sowed, The Signal of Self* are a few other poems which shed light on the thought process of the mind and make us aware of how they are perceived in the outer world and how they can be controlled in the inner mind.

My Own Ride provokes the readers to strengthen the power of determination towards one's destination ignoring all the outer distractions. *The Mistress of Time* is a powerful and beautifully carved poem decorated with plenty of metaphors.

Nothingness in Everything is another poem carrying the essence of life. Though the poems are serious in tone, they comfort and heal the heart of even the laymen. The choice of the symbols and imagery to impart a meaning of reality is very impressive. It evokes an emotional response in the readers not to get swallowed by those obligatory, dark and painful moments of life. The poet's effort in showering a healing touch to the wounded souls suffering from some or the other trauma is really praiseworthy. Reading every poem empowers the soul and inspires to embrace the very colour of life to cherish the seeds of hope.

Wishing all the best for her upcoming creations.

Prabha Khadka
Educator
Kathmandu, Nepal.

Preface

My anthology of poetry titled **As the Darkness Dawns** has been written after my mother's demise. It was also the dark hour when the whole world was succumbed to the deadly virus. The emptiness that emanated my heart based on the happenings and the thoughts within me and around provoked me to pen these dark poems. The simple act of describing something in a new way that has been bothering me gives a whole new perspective helping me to find new ways to handle any kind of complex situation. Pain and darkness are the twins and poetry that encircles around is an avenue for the macabre, the melancholic and the mysterious. For sure, one can experience certain romance in these dark poems which paves the way to enlightenment.

There's something mysterious about that which is hidden and unknown. Much of it is concerned with the darker aspects of the natural world whether, it's the mystery, more abstract or metaphorical kind of darkness. All my poems give rhythm to silence, light to darkness with the magic of metaphor, compactness of expression, use of five senses, simplicity and complexity of meaning in a few lines. The tone in every poem is anxious, contemplative where I am trying to reconcile my identity and deal with darkness. The diction or word power in my poems add depth to my writing.

These poems pay tribute to night or express the burdens of death, suffering, grief and any other negative emotions. To look out of the window when raining, to watch the clouds covering the entire sky and showers of rain sometimes provide dark thoughts opening the door to beauty on the other side of light. Everyone's thoughts and emotions turn dark some time or the other and one of the best ways to safely let that negativity out is to contemplate and experience catharsis through careful introspection. My poems act as a way to release inner feelings and process one's emotions. Each poem is cathartic almost like a form of therapy.

All poems spring from various events of my life that are particularly dark or chaotic. Several people, the kith and kin, the near and dear, the known and unknown I have come across left a mark of darkness in one way or the other. Many controversial and unfortunate situations I have been confronting are expressed in a poetic manner. My poetry presents important insights about mankind's capacity for monstrous acts and also lobby for change. They appeal to the readers' ethical responsibilities and challenge the unspeakableness of dark events by exploring, reanimating or memorialising occurrences and moments that may never be forgotten or silenced.

Reading these poems let the reader see what is weighing on his or her mind, in one's heart which can open door to feelings that are sometimes suppressed until the door is opened. These poems can shine a light on all those dark and hidden crevices of the heart and mind once thought, permanently closed off to the world. The reader may experience as if the world around him or her slows down, makes him or her think, put a spotlight on what the issues might be and forces him or her to logically and methodically answer to it. The poetry aids the reader to find one's own way through metaphorically dark times.

I wish to dedicate this anthology of poems to my beloved and late mother.

Dr Ujjwala Kakarla
Author, Professor, Researcher, Spiritualist

Contents

Nature Intact

Thunder roared bloodthirsty,
The moon and the stars feared
to outshine,
The clouds were feral and the
droplets dried,
The sky was grim and brutal
with its lost beauty,
The birds hurried to their nests,
The wild fauna ceased to roar,
The humanity shivered locked
indoors,
yet the wind didn't stop to blow,
The streams didn't stop to flow,
Nature intact in its resilience,
Its silence seemed hair-raising
and nerve-racking,
For the thunder couldn't threaten
or shake its power.

How Small are our Lives!

I don't want to wait anymore here,

where there's no work to earn.

Looking at the scorching sky in wry,

I want to muse over my dear ones I have left.

I don't need a bus or a truck to travel sahib,

If you set me free, I will risk to walk on foot

to reach my home far off.

How would be my dear ones at home?

Who would be caring my ailing parents?

During this difficult time, if we were together,

We would have happily filled our stomachs with some gruel.

I don't want to wait anymore here

where there's no work to earn.

What a fate! What a fate!

I came so far in search of work for better wages.

The country I live in is so great,

yet, how small are our lives!

I remember those days at home,

Each day, from the first light to twilight,

We worked hard together to fill our starving stomachs;

yet we would forget the hardship in bond of togetherness,

Spreading our smiles and laughter

sitting under the shade of trees.

I don't want to wait anymore here,

Where there's no work to earn.

Is there a bigger disease than poverty?

This pandemic has thrown us in mud breathless.

What a life! What a bad life! what a bitter life!

This is the time, I had to remain

close to my near and dear ones.

Battling with the pandemic,

I want to reach as fast as I could

with a little hope to see them alive.

The Seeds I Sowed

The castle of self,

Stood amid an

infinite garden.

I tilled the soil,

To sow the seeds

I loved.

A few seeds I sowed,

Sprouted into seedlings

and some did not sprout.

These seeds were my

own thoughts.

A few seedlings were

crushed by animals

A few bit the dust,

Unable to cope with

the weather.

Only a few saplings

rose taller and greener,

The revived and the deceased

with their own meaning

Epitomize human evolution

and devolution in grace.

[5]

In the Hell of Darkness

Beneath the same sky,

On the same stage,

variety of plays run in

acceleration to time.

The souls are the same,

but hell, the attributes and roles

race and fight with one another.

Beneath the same sunlight,

In the same theatre,

The characters may differ

on par with situations.

The souls' values are the same,

but hell, the vices and the virtues

are ever in conflict.

Beneath the same moonlight,

In the same darkness,

The speculations in difference

on par with struggles.

Life remains to be the same,

but hell, the dreams and goals

could never be one.

Beneath the same clouds,

In the same nature,

The desires may differ on

par with the thoughts.

Consciousness is the same,

but hell, compassion and deception

are dangerous adversaries forever.

Darkness cannot See its' Own Light

The rain cannot

see its own droplets,

but it quenches

the thirst of every

living thing.

A root cannot

see its own fruits,

but it fills

millions of

hungry stomachs.

The sky cannot

see its own radiance,

but it twinkles

millions of stars

in darkness.

Darkness cannot

see its own light,

but it shows

the path of light

to many blind souls.

The Signs I Discern

Rising up

the waves

feel apart

from the

outer ocean.

Falling down

the waves

feel one

with the

deepest ocean.

Dimming darkness

merges into

dawning daybreak

to embrace its own

brilliance.

Thickening darkness

Breaks off from the

fading daybreak

ignoring its own

brightness.

Breathing in

I create

a meaning

for myself.

Breathing out

I act upon

to analyse

the sign

I discerned.

Those Dark Hours

Those moments

when the known and

the unknown souls,

Took me closer to

grief and death;

yet I survived.

Those moments

when grief

imposed me to

work too hard,

Sucking me down

into fear and despair;

yet I survived.

Those moments

when my own fear

seemed dark,

Closing all the paths

to walk ahead;

yet I survived.

Those moments

when the empty vessels

bellowed their rubbish advice,

Impeding my voice

open to objection;

yet I survived.

Those moments

when I knew...

what I have to do

to make a move,

but ignoring the awful

voices I heard was dicey;

yet I survived.

Those moments

when I knew...

the bad voices can't be quietened,

but awakening with the dreadful

seemed to be day today test papers;

yet I survived.

In the Eyes of the Dark World

In the eyes of the dark world

Learn to walk a little stiffer,

If not, several people will be

waiting as high-speed wind,

To push you down into debris.

In the eyes of the dark world

Learn to act with a little heart of stone,

If you carry a candle like heart

Several people will be waiting,

To burn you into vapour.

In the eyes of the dark world

Learn to act a little tougher,

If not, several people will be waiting,

To make you work like a clock

depleting your energy.

In the eyes of the dark world

Learn to appear a little unwise,

If not several people will be waiting,

To imitate and use your intelligence

leaving you all bankrupt.

The Fictional Creation

After the night leaves,

the dawn of the day comes.

The night remained as it was,

and the day remains as it is.

The date that changes,

makes every day a new day.

The stories that change from time to time,

make the history remain the same.

You may laugh and laugh at it till you get tired,

then shed a few tears and cry in silence

Your laughter gets drenched in your tears

to sparkle once more.

Death that never changes,

alters life in new directions.

The wonder is, you may never feel or see,

Day and night, life and death,

As an illusion of the fictional creation!

A Wooden Boat under the Wild Sky

A creaking wooden boat in the sea,

Roaring like waves to reach the shore,

but the nestlings singing in the nests of canopy,

To the flute of the playful wind.

The boat left alone in the midst of the sea so long,

Wailing under the wild sky unable to find the shore,

but the secrets of the watercraft soaked by the playful waves.

The wild sky and the thick tussles remained still and helpless,

Watching the raging waves carrying the debris on to the

shore,

Leaving the pieces scattered like the broken seashells.

The hounds came howling to the shore with heavy footsteps,

Their dark shade and blood-thirsty eyes resembled the

haunting world,

Amid the evil voices moaning,

The nestlings still singing in the nests of canopy in solace.

My Own Ride

A river's...

Purpose,

Destination

is that ocean

Infinite.

It merges into it,

Becoming the

same ocean,

and the rest

is its own ride.

Life's destiny

has brought me

to such a phase,

Though, I like

some things,

I need a few things,

yet, I don't want

to own any.

The rest has been

my own ride

To cross those

terrible waves,

To reach the shore,

when many I's in me

merge into I,

Becoming an 'I'

As the river and the ocean.

The Chaotic Mind

The mind wants to be happy

but it often thinks of how to be unhappy.

The mind wants to be free of agony

but it repeatedly gets into a tizzy.

The mind doesn't like its own contradiction

but it constantly loses itself in friction.

The mind wants itself to be understood without any words,

but it's not understood the way it wills.

The mind proves its convolution to none,

for it's more often disliked to be believed in by everyone.

As the Darkness Dawns

In the wild night, I heard someone knocking at the door,

I felt aghast and lit the lights, opening the door,

To my surprise, there was no one to trace around.

As I closed the door, I heard the same noise again

Bang... Bang... Bang...Bang…Bang…Bang!!

The knocking didn't cease till the early hours of dawn,

but the door remained closed the whole night.

It's high time, I perceived those to be my silly thoughts

knocking the mind's door.

It's hard to think, feel, imagine, understand and realize,

The depth and intensity of thoughts, emotions,

memories, dreams, words and deeds,

Chasing the mind in the daybreaks.

As the darkness dawns and the mind's door closes,

It's crystal-clear to know, sense, interpret, apprehend and

perceive,

The height of truth and the depth of stability of my inner

Self.

The Bond with the Dirt

The wind carried the leaf into dirt,

While the rain washed off the dirt afar…

floating the leaf above the dirt,

Saving it from losing in the dream of black dirt.

But the leaf's bond with the dirt,

Made the wind blow again in the same direction.

Me this, Me that, invisible speck of dust,

clinging on the wall of head,

When swept with the broom of natural self,

at every moment, and every step of life,

Saves oneself from losing in the dream of black dirt.

But man's bond with the dirt,

Made the speck of dust visible again on the wall of his head.

When the Words Remain Dead

Darkness...

For the sake of

darkness,

Through

darkness,

Gets to

know its' own

darkness,

when the dawn

lights its'

darkness.

Self...

For the sake of

self,

through

self,

Gets to

know its' own

self,

when the

Lotus of Life

revives.

Stillness...

For the sake of

stillness,

Through

stillness,

Gets to

know its' own

stillness,

when uncanny

words remain

dead.

I Gazed at it in Wonder

I saw a glimpse of my thought

when watering the plants.

It was humming a melody in my garden.

I searched her hither and thither,

It was chasing me, blinking its blind eyes.

It moved closer and farther smiling at me

turning formless,

when I stretched my hands to touch it.

After a while, I could feel it forcing

me dead to the world,

but I was flustered with it and it

was upset with me.

I asked my thought,

"Why we were annoyed with each other,

and what bothered it to trouble

me now and then!"

It replied with a wild smile, "I want to

teach you how to live and laugh at your own thought."

I gazed at it in wonder closing my eyes in rumination!

The Signal of Self

When the vehicles

of thoughts

are jammed,

The road of

mind is blocked.

If the path has to

be cleared,

The mind has to

remain poised

for a while.

When the

signal of self

begins to control

the traffic,

Adagio,

the road gets

cleared for

conveyances

to move

on their way.

Although,

the traffic is

controlled,

yet the road

beheld could

never be empty.

Nothingness in Everything

Is there a way where you aren't stuck?

You don't find the way until you stop seeing.

Is there a way out where you are stuck?

you don't find the way until you stop searching.

Is there a way where you haven't been?

you will find the way where you have already stuck.

Is there a way where you get everything?

you will find the way where there is nothingness.

There was everything in the mansion you arrived,

But you could take only nothingness out of everything.

There was nothing in the little hut you didn't want to arrive,

But you could carry everything out of nothingness.

I could Make my Way

I could not catch

those silly leaves

flying and rolling

to the wind,

but I could

make my way

wherever

nature led me to.

I could not catch

those rising

and falling waves

in the sea,

but I could feel life's

joys and sorrows

carrying me

to touch the shore.

I could not catch

those floating and

hovering clouds

in the horizon,

but I could draw on

my wings of imagination

to embrace

the sheltering sky.

As the Darkness Ripens

When the night comes into view

The blue eye turns blackish little by little.

As its darkness ripens...

The third eye sparkles with infinite

tear drops,

Reflecting the ocean of Soul.

When the dawn breaks out

The third eye closes its eyelid in rest.

As the brightness expands...

It drops its' tears on to the earth,

and those that change into dew drops,

Reflect the struggles of soul.

Between the sky and the earth

A drop after drop begins to fall...

The misty sun took off my mind

to a desert

To sprinkle a few wet drops I took in,

To quench the thirst of burning guts.

The Colour of Peace

Each and every home,

In this little village

has a neem tree,

Sheltered from the

sun and the rain.

There's neither a

temple nor a mosque;

I watch over only

small and big gardens

with luxuriant blossoms.

The peasants ploughing in the

fields the whole daybreak,

Look pleasant even in their

toil and sweat.

As the night dawns…

I listen to the sounds

of breeze in all directions.

Some fireflies appear as

waves of light,

and scent of the blossoms

spread as the smoke of incense.

Under the ceiling of the

twinkling sky,

The people rest in silence

on their tiny cots.

All in all, peace...only peace...

That beautiful colour I can't

paint in words.

The Beauty of Surrender

The fallen leaves…

Floating in the stream,

Moving faster than a rowing boat,

Surrendered to the mighty wind.

The fallen flowers…

Scattered on the earth,

Seem more colourful than the sky,

Surrendered to the colourless wind.

The fallen fruits…

Rolling on the soil,

Seem more ripened than the mind,

Surrendered to the raw wind.

That which Ceases not

Distant moon

Seems coming nearer,

Seems going farther,

Like my own destination.

This too seems within the

reach at this moment,

and within the limits

the very next moment.

What seems within my reach

is my own journey of insight,

that which doesn't end,

yet seems closer to my Self.

Playful breeze

Felt close by,

Felt long away,

Like my own mind.

This too makes me feel

closer to my thoughts,

and quite afar from my

crowded feelings.

What I feel within my reach

is my own breath of awareness,

that which ceases not,

yet its rhythm of inhalation and

exhalation may disperse my Self.

I do not Know

Leaving behind

the blue yonder

I do not know

how I fell down

to the earth!

I could not put

a name to...

I was also a star

twinkling in the infinity.

I do not know

how I rolled into

the muddy sack!

The sack is hard

and tied stiffer

I could not see a

way to come out.

I do not know

when the sack is

loosened!

The sack is getting

paler and older

Here and there

I could see the holes

I do not know

how to break out!

Slowly, the sack is

loosening itself

Exerting force on

to push me out.

I do not know

how I reached the

blue all over again!

Isn't the Earth Darker than the Sky?

The night asks the darkness...

Isn't the earth darker than the sky

for all its Washington lights?

Isn't the sky brighter than the earth

despite its pale moon lighting behind

the clouds?

The darkness asks the night...

'Isn't the page of the earth finite even

with unending tales of earthlings?'

'Isn't the page of the sky infinite even

without any tales to narrate?'

The dawn asks the night...

'Isn't the world still asleep even when

the sun is out?'

'Isn't the cosmos awake even when

the moon is out?'

Flow with the Wind of Life

The wind never asks,
"In which direction should
I blow?"
It just blows...
Without knowing its own route!

Nature never asks the wind
to stop blowing
It feels all the mood swings
of the wind,
Without knowing its own fate!

A leaf never blames the wind
for falling down from the twigs
It's coincidental and unwitting
for it to feel the wind,
Without knowing its own state!

How to Accept!

On the day before today

To feel the caprices,

We do not want to feel

might be vulnerable!

We do accept.

On this very day

To feel the whims,

We do not want to feel

might be our tears!

We do accept.

On day-to-day

To feel the waves of life

crashing down,

We do not want to feel

might be a death life!

How to accept...?

We can feel it...

How we are on our way

reaching nowhere!

Feel it hard to accept,

yet we do accept!

We can feel it...
We aren't on any way,
but reach somewhere!
Try to accept...
Nothing belongs to anyone
anywhere,
yet we do not accept!

The Path I Chose

Though
The path I chose

has many stones,

yet I could walk on it

with my fine footwear.

Unnoticed
A few stones got

into my footwear,

and I hardly could put a

step even on the fine path.

Withal
The very path I have been

walking is straight ahead,

and it could be clearly seen,

becoming my memory gently.

Invisible
Twists and turns I anticipated

felt to be the stones visible,

but those existed only in my mind,

becoming my lessons of life.

A Tribute to my Beloved Amma

Amma, I do not want to stand near your grave and weep for
you,
You lead the path, the Almighty laid for you,
Now, I am left with those lovely memories I have of you,
I saw you becoming tired day by day, but your bond of love
didn't let you free for a while,
The Heavenly Father wrapped you in His grace,
Letting you free of the pain you didn't deserve.
You heard His whisper, "Child, come unto the land of peace
and rest",
and you willed to depart from the web of bondage you carved
for this birth
You have been my only strength and support defending me
from the betrayers,
I know how unhappy you were with the wild folk who used
you for their need,
but never showed their gratitude,
I know how secure and happy you used to feel when I was
around you,
You have been a warrior all through your life sacrificing even
the littlest
of your needs,

Your compassion was seen as a weakness to weaken your

mind who you

believed in blindly during my absence,

I am left all alone amid these hypocrites who are seizing even

the little things you have left.

God and I alone know the purpose behind your death,

Amma, I feel your love and embrace much more than when

you were alive!

Ocean of Death

Before entering the ocean of death

Man's mind shakes like a leaf

He wishes to look back at the

paths of attachment, he travelled;

The emotional peaks and valleys, chills and spills,

laughter and tears he has gone through.

When he sees the ocean greeting

in front of him,

He stood aghast thinking of the risk

he has to take to enter the ocean.

yet he could not escape from his own fear of

dissipating into it forever,

as it seemed to be the only way to conquer his fear,

and become one with the death.

Away from the Dry Life

Away from the

hustle and bustle

of city life,

Away from

mechanization

and pollution,

Away from the

dry life and

artificiality,

I arrived my

sweet home at

the countryside.

It's a little haven amid

nature surrounded by

fields and a little stream.

Our pretty garden in the

front yard provides us

fresh vegetables.

Plucking the weeds,

Tilling and watering the

plants seem a fine activity.

Away from everyday

battle of conflicts and

dirty crimes for survival,

An aroma of purity

and naturality makes

life serene and lively.

The Signs of my Window

A single all-round

window in my den,

Oscillated with rapidity,

To the breeze blowing

intense,

that I stood in with

exerting force,

Dragging the doors

to fasten.

I felt as if...

Life is pulling me back

with hurdles alike,

Signalling me,

To make the choices

I need to,

Greeting opportunities

in the offing,

Aiming at the courage

to change,

and get ready for a new

battle.

As I Breathe

As I breathe in

I see myself

as a melted

droplet.

As I breathe out

I see myself

as a blooming

flower.

As I hold my breath

I see myself

Holding soil of life

in my hands.

As I resume to breathe

I see myself

Holding the words that

warble only in the dark.

An Empty Nest

An empty nest was hanging to a tree day and night,

The mother bird left its nest without a word,

The baby birds cried and tried to fly in seek of

their mother.

Some flew with great strength and hope;

A few fell down with their broken wings, hopeless.

The Mother bird migrated to such a land,

where there was neither an origin nor an end,

And the chicks that were alive flew in different directions,

but it was hard to identify the broken wings of the dead birds.

The Mother bird knew not in which direction it flew,

It began staring into the empty space thinking of its baby

birds.

The tree looked desolate awaiting the birds…

In vain, the birds never returned,

but their nest remains stiff still hanging to the same twig.

Money Makes a Man

As long as man is on the earth,
Only money makes him
and takes up to heights,
but man can't take up the
same to the skies,
when the time is to quit the earth.
For some unique folk,
As the money begins to flow,
They tour round and spend on
visiting peaks and palaces,
without a second thought.
When there's hardly any
money left over,
They visit the temples and orphan
homes to donate other's wealth.
As money flows a little more,
Restaurants and farm houses
become the kitchens,
that serve variety of dishes to sate
their appetites;
Megaplex theatres turn to be homes
to relax and entertain themselves.
When time shows its wrath and

sickness knocks at their bodies,

There's scarcely a single penny

left over to spend on their own health.

Essence of Life

I have got something

sufficient for my needs

Why not...?

May be...

Less than what you've,

but I've something to live.

I thought of those who don't

have anything,

and I wished to give some

from what I've.

I felt the essence of life in giving.

You've got everything

More than your wants,

and much more than what others got.

Did you ever think of others?

Did 'much' bring any difference

in your life?

You were busy thinking of yourself,

and you wished to take everything

for yourself,

but you never felt the essence of

life in taking.

If I Could

The dark sky speaks

so much at night,

Solely, a solitary soul

can listen to it.

If I could hear,

A little beyond

If I could fly,

A little further

If I could know,

A little deeper

I feel,

My delusions to be

illusions!

These dark delusions

Success, failure

Positivity, negativity

Winning, losing

Rising, falling

Hope, hopelessness

Purpose, purposelessness

Seem to be my own

self-deception.

These rusted limitations

Pride, ego

Envy, jealousy

Lust, greed

Hatred, enmity,

If polished into

Love, and

Good wishes,

Awareness is what

I embrace.

If I could see myself,

A little keener

If I could judge myself,

A little harder

If I could criticize myself,

A little bitter

If I could guide myself,

A little higher

If I could test myself,

A little tougher

Awareness is what

I realize.

The Mistress of Time

It's during that auspicious

hour,

She wakes embracing

her mother, the sky.

She gazes at her sister,

the dark night,

still nestled in her arms.

Both emerged from the

same womb,

yet her complexion,

Pure and white as ocean waves,

The only princess of

spiritual wealth.

She's the mistress of time,

Reminds humans of limited

hours on the earth,

but only a few could feel her

beauty and light.

It's during that rosy hour,

The daughter of Cosmos,

Comes riding on her white

chariot of clouds,

Chasing the evil spirits and

spreading her cheer.
Her light gives sight to
human eyes,
when evil spirits hide
from her sight.
Her might inspirit the
human mind and senses,
Bringing life to mankind.
She's the mistress of time,
Reminds humans of limited
hours on the earth,
but only a few could feel
her beauty and light.

Persona

Before we knew

our portion,

Life chose us,

We chose life.

We didn't leave

out to choose

Persons

Tussles

Nodus

Nuisance

Malaise.

Surprisingly,

We painted our

own persona,

without a

finishing touch,

and still

we're thinking

holding the brush.

My Own Truth

I dip

my pen

into my

own

emotions

to ink

my own

'truth'

into my

stories.

I am away

from the

'Ego Trap'

of my own

'truth'

to put down

others.

I fall into

my ego

trap in

voicing

my truth

only

when a

'Poisonous

Arrow'

pierces

into my

heart.

The Clay Lamps (Diyas)

Even the daybreaks seem darker…

Every second shows the signs of a nightmare

Moving bodies look to be marionettes,

Free-flowing feelings sense to be upsets.

The glory of existence appears to be overweary,

but the sun is cheery and mighty as ever,

and its brightness is evincing the

strangest things, the eyes never viewed.

The nights seem scarier…

The moon fears to come into sight,

The moonlight is as pale as the starlight,

and the stars are hanging back the clouds eerie.

Seeing the earth lit with millions of diyas.

The sky has fallen in love with the earth,

That's glittering brighter than

the moonlight and trillions of stars.

Only the wind is jealous, disrupting

the clay lamps here and there;

and the lamps struggling to defend

their brilliance,

Reflect the human souls, battling with

their own lives.

Language of Solitude

After several nights of rainfall,

In my window, I see only water

covering all around.

The sunken earth in wetness,

getting wetter with little apricity,

but the half-sunken grass smiles

brighter than before ahead of!

The wind sounds just as it is,

and nature remains still as ever

even in the storm,

but the komorebi entrapped in the

dark clouds is little seen.

Here we are in the present,

there we are in the future!

It's so serene even in chaos!

If the soul slips into the days

like these,

where there is only a language

of solitude to feel,

I rest here in solace making peace

my dwelling place.

Sense of Identity

In the dark hours,

How calmly the snow

rests upon the earth,

Concealing its identity!

It lays its white carpet...

that looks brighter than the moonlight.

The earth under the carpet,

Shivering and struggling for breath,

Battling in the clutches of deadly snowfall,

Lives and relives every second

in losing its identity,

Till the snow melts away

slowly to the wintry sunlight.

I caught sight of the death

approaching me to embrace

in its bosom like a shot.

I felt it like a snow flake,

spine chilling my being

on a wintry night.

I truly lived and relived

in losing my sense of identity,

as I fought to escape from

it every moment.

When I wanted to submit

myself after a long battle,

It vanished all of a sudden

leaving my identity to myself.

All that Season Does

Winter starts

to chill the air

until the earth

and the trees

turn bald.

It's stolen by

the hum of

falling snow

and fire side

tales,

Underneath

the gleam

of lamp-light.

All that season

does tells us a

little of something,

Pulling the darkest

recesses of

human mind

into the present.

Ah, there's truth

behind everything

the season does,

That which can be

experienced only

in silence.

[65]

The Passing Hour

The hour hand is
ticking in fast pace,
yet the time is
moving illimitable.
Each passing hour is
passing into the past,
Just as every wave is
slipping into the ocean.
All the thoughts,
the mind is gathering
and the words that
are gushing forth,
Beyond where the
waves are moving,
Seem to be as distant
as the darkness,
but feel as closer as
its moonlight.

Colourless Droplets

It was airing itself sky-high

Blinding my eyes sometimes

Blocking my nose at times

Deafening my ears now and then.

Rain, and once again you drizzled

your pretty drops down,

After awaiting long hours, I could

hear your unspoken words!

O' Rain, I laughed at the dust that's

left with little strength,

It ceased dancing to the playful wind,

falling swiftly to the ground,

Sticking itself to my feet, down to the earth.

So colourless are these falling droplets to look at,

but how colourful and vibrant

they make the earth and nature!

These droplets resting hither and thither

on petals, leaves, twigs, tussocks…
Seem like God's eternal painting.

An Invisible Spark

I am an

invisible spark

of decisiveness,

Creating

my own emptiness

and fullness of life.

These formless

elements of self

either cause or end

the battle of strife.

There is quicksand

all around to suck

my will of effort.

It seems quite darker,

as I feel my baggage heavier.

Unless I lighten my weight

of feeling deeper,

I can't walk towards

the open seas lighter,

Even, I can't fly towards

 the open skies freer.

I am an invisible spark of

decisiveness to burn

or light my own will.

In Pursuit of Nothing

In pursuit

of wants

All I want

is nothing.

In pursuit

of nothing

All I want

is something.

In pursuit

of something

All I want

is everything.

In pursuit

of everything

All I want

is losing.

In pursuit

of losing

All I want

is gaining.

In pursuit
of gaining
All I want
is nothing.

Instruments Of 'I'

There are words that are not mine

There are words that are mine

but every word vibrates to melt away.

There are thoughts that are not mine

There are thoughts that are mine

but every thought vibrates to melt away.

There are feelings that are not mine

There are feelings that are mine

but every feeling vibrates to melt away.

There's a voice that's not mine

There's a voice that is mine.

but the voice that vibrates never melts away.

Without these things I am no one

Without 'I' these things have no instrument to vibrate.

The Sky's Tears

When the sky

sheds its tears,

The earth smiles

in wetness;

Nature blooms

afresh

in colours of rainbow.

The birds set out

singing;

Nestlings falling

from the nests,

Begin flapping their

wings in hope to fly.

The tear drops,

Beating my window

in rhythm,

Low and high...

as my own thoughts,

want my heed,

To listen to secrets

of my own self.

The Wind and the Glass Pane

"I have to carry so much of dust

you bring in every day,

and bear the bites of the flies and insects

that crawl and rest making me their bed,"

cried the unbroken glass to the wind.

The wind blew hard and broke a little

part of the glass pane,

The fallen pieces wounded many feet that

passed through;

The tender hands cut and bled profuse when laid,

The curses of the victims were more than it could tolerate.

It cried again to the wind, "The unbroken form of mine was

better than the broken form;

but you ruined me into a villain burying my heroism."

The turbulent wind broke the whole glass clearing

the clutter of broken promises...!!!

Eternal Soul

Awaiting,

the whole night

for the sun to shine,

I am in awe...

To see millions

of bodies,

Struggling only to die.

Awaiting,

the whole day

for millions of stars

to twinkle,

I am in awe...

To see my own soul,

Twinkling in quietude,

only to live.

The Beauty in Melting Signs

I feel some situations

meaningful,

and some meaningless.

What provokes

me to create

these signs,

I Know not!

At some point

of time, I felt…

Unless I act upon

these signs,

I can't explore

the secrets of

the Universe.

What I realized

from the most is…

Those signs

that seemed

unfavorable

to meet my wants,

turned to be

more meaningful;

and those that

have been more

favorable,

meeting my wants,

turned to be little

meaningful.

Sometimes, I feel…

these signs melting

like snow in silence.

It's the very beauty

that inspires me

more than a

meaningful sign.

Love that Loves only Truth

I do not

want to

connect

with the

creator

the way

you want

to connect.

My mind

isn't dark

as yours.

I do not

want to

please the

creator

the way

you want

to please.

My heart

isn't dark

as yours.

Love that's

slave to lies

but blind

to truth

ain't the love

God falls for.

He gravitates

to such a love

that loves

only truth.

I Feel

These flowers appear

So colourful

yet natural.

So delightful

yet calmful.

So beautiful

yet soulful.

So teamful

yet peaceful.

So liberal

yet blissful.

Blooming solely

to the falling dew.

These brainy beings appear

So colourful

yet awful.

So brightful

yet terrible.

So beautiful

yet painful.

So artificial

yet showful.

So liberal

yet lustful.

Fading dreadful

under the dark sky.

The Empyrean of Freedom

There were neither

the white nor grey

clouds to trace,

Even there were no

thoughts to race,

still, the mind exists

as it is like the

wide yonder.

These clouds can't

float without

the earth's roof,

Even these thoughts

can't blot without the

mind's proof,

but the mind exists

all alone like

the empyrean of

freedom as a reminder.

The Human Tree

The human tree

is trembling,

To the fierce wind

of pandemic.

Sickened bodies

are collapsing

faster like the

feeble leaves.

Still, a few

strong leaves

are clinging to

the twigs,

Awaiting calmly

resting in the

promises of spring.

As I fix my senses

on the oath of

existence,

The vicissitudes

of the seasons

it instructs,

Recall me to feel

my own strength

of faith knotted in

love of solitude.

I Stop not to Question

Perhaps, some questions

do not have answers,

yet I stop not to question.

My keenness implores me

to wait for a while,

Even after a long wait...

I explore nothing,

I feel only embarrassed,

Time seems poignant

slipping into voidness,

Still I do realize my own

freedom in extra miles

of questioning!

It is here the truth

of life is concealed,

Awaiting me not to instruct

but only to enlighten.

The World of Deception

The tree of

honesty,

Left behind

defunct,

In this wild

world of

deception.

The flowers of

opportunities

that are

plucked,

Fade faster

losing their

beauty of

triumph.

They seem

painted

just in dark

colours,

Delightful to

the peepers.

The Night Sky

The night Sky
Couldn't find the
tiny lights,
but could hear the
whispers of stars.

The night Sky
Could see the
moon,
but couldn't hear
its whisper.

The night Sky
Couldn't feel the
murmur of stars,
though they were
countless, crowded.

The night Sky
Could feel the moon's
peaceful smile,
though it was left all
alone amid huge crowd.

I Can't

I can't paint

in words,

That azure sky,

In the black of

the night.

I can't report,

The mood of

the wind,

when it's noiseless,

before I know where I am.

I can't sketch the

twists and turns of life,

when the path

I set foot on is long

and straight.

An Heirloom of Tears

The skyscrapers are burning in the fire;

the cities are drowning in the tempest;

the twigs of the giant trees are breaking

to the dust devil;

the birds are fleeing off from the smashed nests,

but man, alone is lost in the sand dunes of desires.

Wholly immersed in the waves of dreams,

his sight is nowhere,

His signature of sleep on the paper of eyes,

His dumbness of silence on the mike of lips

Haunt as his own memories from time to time

Begging for an heirloom of tears quite awful

to chew over!!!

A Natural Link up

Who runs for whom?

Who greets whom?

This meeting that…

That greeting this…

How naturally this links up with that!

A touch without a

prologue and an epilogue!!!

The day doesn't run for the sun,

but the sun flashes to meet the day.

The day greets it wholeheartedly,

with a touch of wonderful link up!!!

The night doesn't run for the moon and stars,

But the moon glows and the stars flicker to meet the night.

The day greets them in jouissance,

with a touch of eye-catching link up!!!

Nature doesn't run for the spring,

But the spring comes into view to embrace nature.

Nature greets it in solace,

with a touch of alluring link up!!!

Desire doesn't run for man,

but man is enthralled to keep it under lock and key.

Desire greets man in enticement,

With a touch of charismatic link up!!!

Who runs for whom?

Who greets whom?

This meeting that…

That greeting this…

How naturally this links up with that!

A touch without a

prologue and an epilogue!!!

The Sky is Dancing Everywhere

The sky looks charming

with its trillions of stars,

but the earth looks melancholic

with its billions of earthlings.

The earth knows nothing of

its habitants,

but the sky knows well, the

unending stories on the earth.

The earth has no role to play

in the cosmos,

but the sky knows well, its'

role on the earth.

The sky is a divine setting of

solace for the hearts that are worn,

but the earth is a romantic realm

for the minds that are wise.

The earth seems moving everywhere,

but nowhere to go,

The sky seems floating to nowhere,

but it's dancing everywhere.

At that Eerie Moment

As the sun rested

in nature's lap,

The darkness leaks from

the bosom of the sky,

and the night queen sat on

its' throne of emptiness

when this darkness seemed

like the end!!!

At that eerie moment

the moon woke up,

Hurrying past the realm of night,

Fitting in the bosom of the sky

in wholeness,

To beautify the darkness ripening,

when the end seemed to be the

new beginning!!!

The waves that Fall for the Ocean

The beautiful moments

slip away like those

tiny and large waves,

but the memories remain

still like a closed ocean.

These memories fall for

those moments over and again,

Like those waves that fall

for the ocean.

Some waves touch the shore;

Some stuck up in the middle of the ocean;

some never reach the shore.

As the ocean and the waves

flow at their own pace,

so too, the time and life flee away

at their own will,

that never return in the same form

to feel the same old touch!!!

A Pointless Hunt

Not knowing from where the

fragrance emanated,

The musk deer stood still

feeling its own aroma.

Being unaware of its own scent

that emerged from within,

It ran in every direction it could,

but its hunt was pointless…fruitless!!!

A falling star was searching

for the sky,

Failing to recall the direction

to look up,

It felt only the earth's dust everywhere,

when coming closer to it.

Still, it was tireless of searching its' abode,

Being unaware of crashing in no time…no time!!!

Life's Vision

Even the paths are tired,

To bear the heavy tramp of

thousands of feet,

For bye, the growing murmur of their

deep voice echoing in the air.

The paths are now quieter trying to

understand life,

Life in turn perceiving the wounds of the

paths to walk gentler and more cautious.

The dust of intersection may blur

the eyes of life,

when life has to change itself

first and foremost,

To clear its' vision of destiny prior to

changing the path.

My Own Want

A thought that stems in me,

Makes me wonder to know about

its seed.

Before I could explore its origin,

It grows into a sapling of want.

The very want creates in me a

want to know its roots.

Even before, I finished digging the mud,

The want pulls diverting me to obtain that want.

As I lift my arms to pluck that want,

My hands fail to reach its height,

At times, the want I pluck slips off afar, invisible.

As much as the want intensified,

I failed to get that want.

As I recall, I forgot to know about my want

before stretching to get it,

I become detached of my want magnetizing

the bliss of patience,

when the very want flows towards my

direction to embrace!!!

Sinking Man

The wind isn't dumbstruck,
To see the seasons changing
Slow-paced.
It's startled to see ou changing
swifter than the seasons!!!

The tree isn't staggered,
To see its fruits falling
when ripened.
It's shocked to see oom picking
even its fallen fruits!!!

The sea isn't astonished,
To see its waves sinking
the giant ships.
It's dumbfound to see man
sinking in his vicious waves!!!

The earth isn't flabbergasted,
To see its stones feelingless.
It's non-plussed to see its earthlings devoid
of feelings left with just named relations!!!

Mind in Anticipation

In the early hours of dawn,

Nothing accompanies

Neither the day's manipulations

nor the night's gullible dreams.

A slight anger caresses me

when I look at myself again!!!

For all that, I am not frightened

of sunset nor of darkness,

but I fear others' dark thoughts,

If spread as a plague sickening the body

and confusing my own mind in darkness!!!

Dr. Ujjwala Kakarla

Author, Educator, Researcher, Spiritualist

Profile

Dr. Ujjwala Kakarla holds her doctorate in English Literature. She has been the Professor of English in various technical institutions for fifteen years. She also served as senior linguist expert at aviation sector in Hyderabad. She is an educator who imparts her training in English Language, Communication and Soft Skills, Human Values and Professional Ethics and Creative Writing. She is a published author of several books. A good number of her articles and research papers have been published in national and international journals of repute, and holistic magazines. She is also a passionate researcher in multidisciplinary aspects viz, Psychology, Philosophy, Spirituality, Indian and Western Literature. She loves writing, reading, researching, painting, learning new languages and art of contemplation. The finest aspect of her personality lies in self-exploring the eternal beauty and mystical secrets of spiritual self. As an author and educationist, she is a recipient of Nation Choice Award.